MIDNIGHT PASS

A NOVELLA

D1713827

TODD CAMERON

SHARK ISLAND PRESS

MIDNIGHT PASS

SHARK ISLAND PRESS

First Edition Publishing October 2021

SHARK ISLAND PRESS
PO Box 326
Englewood, Florida
34295

Author photo: Valerie Vitale

Cover design and interior formatting by:
King's Custom Covers
www.KingsCustomCovers.com

ISBN: 979-8496742597

Printed in the United States of America

31 30 29 28 27 26 25 24

For Valerie—many more moonlit midnights.

"Do you not know that there comes a midnight hour when everyone has to throw off his mask?"

—Søren Kierkegaard

"The monster showed up just after midnight. As they do."

—Patrick Ness

"WTF: Welcome To Florida."

—Anonymous

MIDNIGHT PASS

March 14, 2022
Englewood, Florida

The sun had sunk behind the Gulf and a twilight of deep lavender was falling across Manasota Key. The late winter days were lengthening and warming quickly, the evening air hovered in the high seventies. Florida in March was the peak of the season for those escaping the long northern winter; the snowbirds were already here, having flocked down in the fall months, now the tourists were visiting in droves, and it was also the height of spring break. The town of Englewood, due to its off the beaten path location, remained a more quaint and quiet area, retaining a true Old Florida atmosphere, still carrying the vibe and memories of a once sleepy fishing village.

Twenty-three-year-old Haley Wolfe was on her spring break from Columbia University, but tonight she was far from celebrating a rite of college life with her friends in Miami Beach. Haley sat on the back porch of her grandmother's rented small one-bedroom bungalow, looking out on Lemon Bay. For the third time she put down the novel she was trying to read. Haley's thoughts were on her aging ninety-year-old grandmother Joan.

Haley had come down to Florida from New York not to party on South Beach, but to visit and assist her grandmother. Joan was elderly, frail, and not in the best of health. For the past few years, she had been having a caregiver come and stay with her in the evenings to help with dinner, meds, and her bedtime routine. What was currently even more dire than Joan's health was her finances. She was running out of funds, slowly depleting her small savings down to nothing with her expenses; chiefly the $1400 a month rent for the bungalow.

Haley had run over her grandmother's finances, and Joan had about two months left before she would have to leave her bungalow, move into a cheaper place and lose the caregiver. This past weekend Haley had checked out an assisted living facility for seniors in Joan's adjusted budget—but she simply could not picture her grandmother living in there. Haley had no idea what she was going to do. As a full-time student working pick-up shifts at a Starbucks in Harlem, she certainly did not have any money to help, and neither did her mother. Haley's mother was out on Long Island, divorced, drinking heavily, and living paycheck to paycheck herself. Her father was long gone and had been out of the picture for years.

Haley set aside the novel she was trying to lose herself in— *Heat Lightning*—a Florida noir thriller by bestselling author John Cannon. She looked out across the drum smooth bay to Sandpiper Key. A brief of pelicans swooped low across the flats and settled together on the mangroves to roost for the night. From across Beach Road, she could hear the muted beat and thrum of live music. Inside the bungalow, the caregiver, a pleasant woman in her late sixties, would be with her grandmother for the evening. Haley had been in town since Friday, this was her fourth night in Florida, and the pace of the Englewood Beach Villas retirement community was gratingly slow. The seniors ate dinner at 4 p.m., turned in by eight, and the highlight of the day was who won the morning's shuffleboard game.

On an impulse decision, Haley rose and set out through the maze of white bungalows, heading towards the front gates of the bungalow complex. Her attire was casual, a simple white T-shirt emblazoned with ENGLEWOOD BEACH in flamingo pink block letters—a gift from her grandmother that naively stamped 'tourist' on Haley's forehead—jean shorts, and navy-blue Vans, no socks.

Haley was a pretty girl, standing about five six, slim and fit, with dirty blonde hair falling just past her shoulders. Her eyes were baby blue, bright, and kind, and her skin was a creamy white. She graduated high school as an honors student on the Dean's List and gained acceptance to Columbia on a scholarship. That was the only way she had made it into the Ivy league school, her family, consisting of just her mother and grandmother, certainly did not have the money for tuition. Despite being book smart Haley was lacking in street smarts, having grown up in a sheltered area of Long Island.

She crossed Beach Road at the roundabout, circling around the massive steel conch shell sculpture, and headed towards the sound of the music. On this Monday evening during the high season SandBar Tiki & Grille was packed with a mix of locals, vacationers, snowbirds, and a handful of scattered younger spring breakers. The band was playing a decent cover of Bon Jovi's "You Give Love a Bad Name".

Haley threaded her way into the open-air beach bar, the entrance and grounds marked by flaming tiki torches, the flooring plank boardwalks laid on hard-packed sand. Approaching the first of two bar areas, she passed a large eight-foot-tall wood carving of a pirate resembling the infamous Captain Morgan. The teak and bamboo bar stretched long to one side, covered by sun-faded palm fronds. SandBar's motif was pure Polynesian culture, playing off as a watering hole in the South Pacific, while being situated on the Gulf Coast of Florida.

It all seemed to work; the energy was high, the atmosphere fun and relaxed, and the joint was at capacity with people eating, drinking, and moving to the music on the dance floor in front of the band.

MIDNIGHT PASS

Haley scanned the bar for an opening, saw one at the far end, and made her way over. She slipped by a line of patrons into the last spot beside a darkly tanned, well-dressed couple somewhere in their fifties. Haley was surprised when it only took one of the bartenders, a blonde girl about her age, just a moment to see her, swing down the lounge, slip a coaster on the bar, and ask her what she would like to drink.

Haley had already checked out the chalkboard cocktail list and went for a drink she recognized but had never tried. "I'll try a Mai Tai."

The bartender smiled. "Sure—one Mai Tai."

As the girl hustled away to fix her drink Haley looked over SandBar some more. The band played at the back along the water's edge under a large tiki hut. At least forty tables, all full tonight, were set about under parasol shades and strings of lights, tied between coconut palms. The second tiki bar was further back and off to one side, along the waterfront of Chadwick Cove, a small nook in Lemon Bay in the backside of Manasota Key. Underwater dock lighting created a deep green ambience, and a few mid-size boats were moored along the bar's wharf, their hulls shimmering emerald.

Her drink arrived in a lowball glass and Haley sipped the quintessential cocktail of the Tiki culture; rum, Curaçao liqueur, orgeat syrup, and lime juice. The drink was tart, citrusy, and refreshing. She was halfway through the beverage, enjoying the music—the band was now on "Wanted Dead or Alive"— and feeling the rum work when she made eye contact with a guy who had just walked in through the tiki torch entrance.

Haley immediately found him quite attractive. He looked to be a few years older than her, late twenties, cleanshaven, tanned, tall but not too tall, looking extremely fit in a dark and wild patterned Floridian shirt, burgundy cargo shorts, and sandals. He had dark brown hair, almost black, cut short and styled. Haley's heart sped up a few beats when he gave her a direct and engaging smile. She smiled back, but broke the connection first, dropping her eyes back to her drink.

After a beat and another sip of her Mai Tai, she cast a furtive glance over, and watched as he greeted and chatted with a couple of people he knew. Haley's heart did another pick-me-up when he looked over again and started to make his way directly towards her.

She took another good pull on her cocktail, hopes split evenly—that he would either abort his approach or continue over to her. She looked up and smiled politely as he neared. He passed behind her and circled around, taking a position at the perpendicular end of the bar, his right arm just inches from her left. He smelled clean with a hint of spice. As amusing as this was, Haley had no interest beyond some casual bar banter. She was single and had not been seeing anyone in over a year; her focus was school, and she was down here to sort out the current family crises.

"Hi." His grin was big, his body language open, his confidence high.

"Hey," Haley replied, against her better judgement giving him a coy smile.

"I came over for two reasons: one, you're beautiful and caught my eye—and two, I can see you're clearly not from Florida . . . so I have to ask, where are you from?"

Haley turned a deaf ear to the compliment. She had been hit on dozens of times before. She twisted her face into a questioning smile, "What gave it away?"

"Well, again, two things, you've got northern skin, and that shirt—nobody who lives in town, or possibly the state for that matter, would wear that shirt."

Haley remembered she was wearing the T-shirt her grandmother had given her when she arrived, a gift from the Barefoot Trader souvenir store. Chagrined, she glanced down at the front of her shirt. "Well, I'm from New York. Long Island to be more accurate."

"Oh yeah? My family has a summer home on Long Island, in Southampton."

Haley nodded, not reacting, or caring, if he was trying to impress her. "I'm from Glen Cove."

Now he nodded, extended a hand, and said, "I'm Sean."

Haley paused for only a moment, then shook his hand—his grip was warm and firm. "I'm Haley."

"Happy to meet you, Haley from Glen Cove. Welcome to Florida."

"Thanks," Haley smiled, and took a sip of her drink.

The blonde bartender came over to serve Sean, and he looked at Haley's glass. "Are you having another?"

Haley considered; the bar was an enjoyable scene, Sean seemed easy-going and harmless, and she certainly was not planning on going back over to her grandmother's place anytime soon.

"Sure," she replied.

"Two Mai Tai's," Sean told the bartender. He turned back to Haley, "So what's brought you down from Long Island to Florida? Besides our weather?"

Haley raised her eyebrows; she certainly wasn't going to go into too much with this guy. And she was paying for her drink. "I'm just visiting family."

"You're not down with any friends?"

Haley shook her head.

"Englewood's not really a big party spot," said Sean.

"I'm not here to party," Haley replied.

"That's good, because SandBar's pretty much it for nightlife around here."

Their drinks came and they each savored the cocktails. The band was hard into "Raise Your Hands" and a high energy coursed the beach bar. Haley was settling in, relaxing. The SandBar was entertaining; great music, a heavenly drink, and a rather attractive individual who wasn't coming on too strong or annoying, yet. She gave Sean another glance. The shirt he was wearing was downright hip barbarian—a short sleeve black button down with a pattern of luminescent pink flamingoes and purple machine guns.

"That's a pretty cool shirt," Haley commented.

Sean grinned. "Isn't it? Thanks—I saw the company on Instagram—you should see the other ones they have. Really boss." He sipped on his Mai Tai. "How long are you in town for?"

"A week. I'm on spring break, from Columbia."

"Nice. What're you majoring in?"

"Environmental and Earth Sciences."

"Hmm—there's a lotta work of that kind here in Florida. Is this your first time down here?"

"Yeah."

"What do you think?"

"Of Florida? Not sure yet, I've only been here three days. I do love wearing shorts in March though. Are you from here?"

"Native, born and raised." Sean took another sip of his drink and steered the conversation back to Haley. "What family are you staying with?"

"Just my grandma. She's older, not in the best of health anymore unfortunately."

"I'm sorry to hear that. So, you're spending the week with her?"

Haley nodded. "Yep."

"Are you gonna have time to do anything fun while you're here? Other than hang out at SandBar drinking Mai Tai's and listening to a Bon Jovi cover band?"

Haley laughed. "Maybe."

Sean was likely going to ask her out, to get together this week. She saw that coming. He was local, came from money, with a family home in Southampton. Handsome, clean-cut, a sporty dresser. While she was here her evenings were pretty much hers, as her grandmother's caregiver arrived around 4 p.m. each day and stayed until Joan went to bed.

Through the bar they had a view of the water, and a boat was approaching, a center console Boston Whaler with two couples onboard. The Whaler eased into the dock, and moored up, the couples stepping off to make their way to the tiki bar at the back of SandBar.

Haley made an impressed expression. "I've never seen anyone take a boat to a bar before."

Sean nodded slowly. "Neat, huh? There's a lotta great spots on the water around here." He took another swig of the rum drink, and asked, "Would you like to get out on a boat while you're here?"

Haley considered the lead, and nodded, "That would be fun."

"I have a boat, if you'd like, I can take you out?"

Haley looked at Sean, reading his face, his eyes. It was a sincere offer. An open opportunity to spend some time on a boat in Florida with a damn good-looking guy. She would be silly not to go. "That sounds fun."

Sean beamed. "Alright. How about this time tomorrow night?"

"At night?" Haley asked. She was a bit surprised it would be at night, but the time suited her well with her evenings free.

"Yeah, the Gulf is incredible at night, and the boat has some really cool lighting."

After a moment Haley agreed. "I'm in. Where?"

"There's a dock at Blind Pass Park, it's just a five-minute ride from here, up the Key. I can pick you up there with the boat."

Haley thought this over for a moment. She could easily grab an Uber to this park . . . if it was only five minutes away it was just outside of town. Nodding, she said, "OK Sean, you're on. A boat ride tomorrow night."

Sean grinned, "Super. And I promise—it's just a three-hour tour."

Haley laughed aloud. "Alright skipper."

They spent the next hour sharing another Mai Tai, talking, joking, laughing. At ten o'clock Haley said she had better get going home, and they ended the night agreeing again that Sean would pick her up at 9 p.m. tomorrow at the Blind Pass Park dock. She walked back over to the Englewood Beach Villas more than a little rum-buzzed, giddy, and excited for what tomorrow night might bring.

＊ ＊ ＊ ＊

At five to nine the next night Haley's Uber driver turned off Manasota Key Road and pulled into Blind Pass Park. The park was a sandy isthmus surrounded by mangroves that backed into Lemon Bay, providing a shelled parking lot for the beach. It was indeed just five minutes up the winding, twisting canopy road on the barrier island, but the first thing Haley noticed was how dark and deserted it was. There wasn't a single other person around and there were no lights at all.

"Where's the dock?" she asked the driver.

The Uber driver was a brisque heavyset woman in her late forties. "You wanna go to the dock?"

"Yes," replied Haley.

"You didn't tell me that," the driver said, pulling forward. "The docks at the back of the parking lot."

The car's headlights splashed across an empty parking lot and thick mangroves. A minute ahead there was a sign for a kayak launch to the right. The driver went left, pulled into a gap in the mangroves, and brought the car to a stop. Through the windshield a blue and white reflective county park sign read: Blind Pass Park Public Dock. Haley used the app to leave a tip, thanked the driver and got out. As the Uber pulled away, tires crunching on the crushed shell, the night closed in.

The air was warm and humid, with a brackish smell. To the west Haley could hear the waves on the beach rushing in, rolling surf on sand. Overlapping frog calls permeated the night with their hypnotic sounds. The sky was clear, and the stars twinkled brilliantly, the moon sitting directly overhead, bright enough to cast shadows, only three days out from full. Haley's eyes adjusted and the darkness shrank back some.

Using the light from her phone, she made her way forward slowly, up a path cut through the mangroves. She came upon a wood-plank boardwalk, and holding her light high, carried on. The boardwalk traversed through the growth, coming out on the waters of Blind Pass and a large dock. The solid dock was constructed of wide plank and thick pilings and stretched more than a hundred feet along the side of the pass, backed by a wall of mangroves.

There was no sign of a boat, so she walked the length of

the dock, listening to the night sounds. The water was dark and alive with activity, little splashes, and swirls . . . black drum, redfish, a passing bonnethead shark. To the west, towards the backside of the beach, was a dead end of shallow flats, but to the east the pass opened into the expanse of Lemon Bay, and Haley could see a few lights on the far aside, just shy of a mile across.

A few mosquitoes found her, whining around Haley's ears. She swatted them away and checked her phone. 9:04 p.m.

Haley walked the dock to keep the mosquitoes and no-see-ums at bay. Tonight, she had dressed a little more to impress, but also knowing she was going out on a boat, kept it casual. She wore a V-neck floral print blouse, sage twill shorts, and her Vans. Haley was not a girl to wear much makeup, but she had added a touch of mascara and lipstick before heading out.

At 9:11 with the no-see-ums nipping at her ankles Haley was having her first thoughts that Sean might be a no-show. Bending to swat her calf she decided that at a quarter after she was going to call back that Uber.

Two minutes later, squatting again to slap an ankle, her eye caught a light out the pass, and she looked up and saw a boat in Lemon Bay. A large boat, a yacht. Bathed in violet lighting and heading north up the bay.

She stood and watched as the yacht slowed, and then the bow started to turn in her direction, heading into Blind Pass. As the boat approached it became apparent just how big the vessel was. Haley did not know much about boats, but, if this was Sean, this was not at all what she was expecting him to show up in.

The Bertram yacht was sixty-one feet of sleek and classic lines, sporting a crisp white deep-V hull, a metallic black tint wraparound salon window, massive command flybridge, and more than fifteen feet of beam. The entire stern cockpit and flybridge were bright with neon violet accent lighting, and lights below the waterline had the bay surrounding the yacht glowing an ambient magenta. The craft's twin engines rumbled deeply, churning up the waters, as the boat was expertly sidled up to the mooring, bumping lightly on dropped fenders. Across the transom in large black and gold lettering was her name, *Midnight Pass.*

Haley stood in semi-shock, taking a step back, as the yacht settled in on the dock.

"Sorry I'm a bit late!" Sean called from the helm up on towering flybridge.

Haley looked up, let out a short incredulous laugh and shook her head. "You've got to be kidding?"

Sean was looking down at her, flashing a wide grin, his face cast a deep violaceous hue. He finalized the docking procedure and shifted the engines into neutral. Sean swung himself from the bridge, scuttling down a ladder and dropped to the deck. He leaned across the port gunwale and held out a hand. "Step aboard, she'll sit here for a bit—there's no current in the pass and we're at slack high tide."

Slipping her cell phone into the back pocket of her shorts and taking Sean's hand Haley stepped over the gunwale and onto the teak decking.

"Welcome aboard," Sean said, holding her hand for a few moments longer than necessary. He was in another wild black Floridian style shirt, this one emblazoned with a pattern of glowing, cyan-colored octopuses and anchors. The top three buttons were open showing a tanned and nicely shaped chest.

"Thanks," Haley replied. Her eyes traveled from Sean around the spacious cockpit and up the rear of the command flybridge. "All right . . . when you said boat, I thought you meant like a fishing boat."

"This is a fishing boat, it's a sport-fisher, a convertible actually."

Haley looked Sean in the eye, a smirk on her face. "This isn't your boat."

He laughed. "No, it's not. It's my father's. It's his pride and joy. But don't worry—you're safe. I can handle it better than he does. C'mon up on the bridge."

Haley, still in a state of shock and awe over the yacht, followed Sean up the ladder to the flybridge. Knowing almost nothing about boating, she stood beside Sean and watched as he powered up the engines and nudged a joystick control. The bow started to swing out from the dock, circling into the dark waters of the pass. The yacht completed a full 180-degree arc, until they were pointing back towards Lemon Bay. Haley felt the engines rumble belowdecks under her feet.

"We're gonna go on a little excursion—I'm going to take us down the bay and out Stump Pass into the Gulf," said Sean.

Haley could not hide her excitement. He throttled up and the Bertram moved effortlessly and smoothly through the calm waters. They settled into the twin padded helm chairs and Haley watched the mangroves slip by on either side.

Coming out into the middle of Lemon Bay, Sean piloted the yacht into the channel. He looked over at Haley and her face told him everything he needed to know; she was relaxed and thoroughly enjoying the night ride, and his company. She caught his look and smiled. Sean grinned, "Are you ready for a ride?"

Haley nodded and Sean throttled up. The twin props caught water and *Midnight Pass* responded, coming quickly to a solid plane. Sean kept it at the intracoastal speed limit, the 88,000-pound yacht slipping down the bay at twenty-five miles per hour. The fuel consumption at this rpm was bringing smiles of delight to the faces of several Saudi princes.

An exhilarating thrill went through Haley, as the warm night air whipped her hair. She watched the barrier island of Manasota Key pass by on their right, and lights from the town of Englewood on their left. *Midnight Pass* slowed up to slip under the Tom Adams Bridge, and in the southern end of the Lemon Bay Aquatic Preserve Sean powered up again. Coming upon The Lighthouse Grill they rounded the channel marker for Stump Pass, and Sean spun the stainless-steel wheel turning the bow due west. The yacht navigated the inlet, coming out onto the open waters of the Gulf of Mexico. The Bertram handled the two-foot swells effortlessly, with only a slight pitch, and no roll due to the modern Seakeeper.

The dark beach fell off their stern, and Haley could see a white line of waves running up onto the sand in the pale moonlight. About 1000 feet offshore Sean ran them back north again, up past Stump Pass Beach State Park and the beachfront homes on Manasota Key.

"Whaddaya think?" Sean asked as they came upon Englewood Beach, the town's main beach, boardwalk, and Chadwick Park. Haley had been quiet for the ten minutes it took them to traverse the bay, and he had let her take in the experience.

Haley turned to him, "It's just incredible." She looked back again at the beach and could see the dark silhouettes of scattered people walking the sand, a few in the water.

"We're just about where SandBar is," Sean said as he dropped the throttle, "It's just on the other side of the beach, across the road."

"Oh . . .!" Haley gathered her full bearings. They had gone south, come out into the Gulf, and looped back north. She had become disoriented on the water, at night, and not knowing the area.

"I'm going to anchor us here for a bit," Sean said. There was a slight west wind of about ten miles per hour. Sean maneuvered the bow offshore and tapped a switch on the console. A clanking rush of chain rang out and then a splash as the anchor plunged into the Gulf. He slowly reversed the Bertram as the rode let out, until the anchor caught firm in the sand bottom, then cut the engines.

The new quiet brought up the sounds of water slapping the hull, and off their stern the steady and constant rush of waves rolling onto the beach. Overhead the clear night sky was a vista of stars, and the brilliant moon made the Gulf sparkle. The air was heavy with the pungent fresh smell of salt. There were no other boats out; to the south, west, and north the horizon was black and to the east the sooty smudge line of Manasota Key held only a smattering of lights.

"Let's head down," Sean said, motioning to the ladder, "Would you like a drink?"

"Sure," Haley agreed, still taking it all in. "The night sky sure doesn't look like this in Manhattan."

"Have you been out to Montauk?"

"A couple of times, when I was a kid."

"It's my favorite part of Long Island."

They descended to the cockpit and Sean slid open a door paned with tinted glass. "C'mon in."

Haley followed him through into the salon and had to suppress a gasp. The interior of the yacht was nothing short of opulent. The entire salon was modern wood and steel, with white ash wide-plank flooring, and backlit with LED recessed lighting. To port a large U-shaped sofa surrounded a teak coffee table that faced a flatscreen TV. To starboard polished barstools lined an expansive white marble top galley, and opposite the galley sat a large teak dining table and chairs, all surrounded by the molded panoramic salon window. The air was dry and cool, and at the fore end steps led down to a carpeted hallway.

Haley let out a breath. "This is . . . nice." She turned to look at Sean. "All right, so what does your father do for a living?"

Sean laughed, "He owns a couple of businesses. What would you like to drink?"

Haley thought Sean was either being modest or deflecting with that answer. "What have you got?"

"Pretty much whatever you like, wine, beer, mixed drinks, or lots of non-alcoholic stuff too, if you like?"

"Ahhhhh, a glass of wine sounds nice. Do you have red?"

"I think we do." Sean tapped a button on a large touchscreen control panel on the starboard bulkhead and music came on—Twenty One Pilots singing "Saturday". He glanced questioningly at Haley, and she smiled. As Sean circled into the galley Haley slid onto one of the barstools. Kneeling below the counter he held up a bottle of red wine with a questioning look.

Haley made a face. "No idea, I'm not a wine connoisseur by any means."

Sean read from the label: "The Prisoner Red Blend—California, 2018." He shrugged. "It looks good—let's give it a shot." He stood, uncorked the bottle, procured two wide-bowled Burgundy glasses, and poured them a third full. He slid one over to Haley and held up his glass. "Cheers to you, Haley, and your first trip to Florida."

"Thank you," Haley smiled.

Their glasses clinked, and they shared a taste of the bold red wine.

"Maybe it won't be your last trip?" Sean asked.

Haley cocked her head to one side. "Mmmm, I don't know."

After a beat, Sean asked, "How is your grandmother doing?"

"The same—not great."

"How old is she?"

"Ninety-one in June."

Sean raised his eyebrows. "That is getting up there."

"It is." Haley sipped her wine. "She lives in the Englewood Beach Villas."

"I know the place . . . right across the street from SandBar."

Haley nodded. "She might have to move out and find a new place."

"Why?"

"The cost, it's adding up. Basically, she can't afford the rent." Haley immediately regretted saying this, not wanting to get into her personal life with Sean.

"Damn," said Sean, "There are lots of places for seniors around town, maybe she can find a cheaper place?"

"Maybe."

"What's her budget?"

"She'll need to find something well under a thousand a month. Under nine would be even better. I've been looking at a few places she can possibly afford. She's not going to like them. Plus, she still needs a caregiver—" Haley stopped herself, pausing for a minute. "Let's talk about something else, OK?"

Sean twisted his lips and nodded once. "No problem. But I'll keep an eye out for something that might work for your grandmother. I'll ask around this week, I've got a few connections. I'm sure there's a place that will work for her."

Haley thought this over for a moment, sipping her wine. This guy was really checking the items off her list quickly; attractive, made her laugh, charming, unexpected surprises, and now showing a caring and compassionate side. "Thanks," Haley said, smiling, "I'd appreciate that."

"Sure thing. So, when do you head back to New York?"

"I fly back home on Friday."

"Three days," Sean taunted, "You better make them count."

"You know, I actually wasn't even planning to come to Florida. My friends are all over in Miami Beach, for the Ultra Music Festival."

"Ultra's an absolute blast. You should have gone."

"I know. It was on the table. But I decided I was going to stay home for the break to work and study . . . then my mom asked me to come down here to Englewood and help my grandma find a new place."

"Your mom asked *you* to come down?"

Haley caught Sean's look. "My mom is in no condition to help her mother—she can barely even take care of herself right now."

Sean nodded and said nothing for a beat. "I have an idea. Why don't we take the rest of this bottle and head out onto the bow?"

Haley nodded. "That sounds like a great idea." She glanced around the salon. "I just need to use the bathroom first—I hope this boat has a bathroom?"

Sean laughed. "It actually has three. But it's called a 'head' on a boat, not a bathroom. The day head is just down those stairs, second door on the right."

"Right," Haley shot him a mocking grin, getting up to make her way forward. "I'll be right back."

The yacht was almost motionless at anchor, but the first glass of wine was going right to her head with a relaxing pleasant buzz. She made her way down a set of LED backlit steps, along a carpeted hallway and opened the second door to starboard. Finding a light switch and flicking it on, she was greeted with a swank bathroom: teak designer cabinetry, porcelain bowl sink, and a spacious stand-up shower with a glass door and teak grated floor. The bathroom was larger, and nicer, than her grandmother's back at the Englewood Beach Villas.

Haley used the facilities, and then checked herself out in the mirror. All was as good as could be. Making her way back into the hallway, she looked aft towards the stairs leading up to the salon and could not see Sean in her line of sight. Unable to resist she popped open the door to her right, at the forward end of the hallway. Inside was the second guest VIP stateroom, décor matching the salon. The bedside lighting was on, highlighting a queen bed, the foot facing her, and the walls converging in the bow behind the headboard. A beautiful bedroom by any standards, and they were on a boat.

Haley bit her lip and smiled self-effacingly, picturing herself and Sean on the bed together. She closed the door softly and made her way back up to the salon, where Sean was waiting with the wine.

* * * *

Sean was a great kisser. Haley learned this an hour and a half later as they sat on the long flat open bow of *Midnight Pass*, their legs dangling over the side. She recognized they were sitting directly over the stateroom she had looked in on. Haley had asked Sean a bit more about himself, but he was not too talkative, always changing tack and flipping the discussion back to her or another topic. She learned he worked for his father, who was the owner of several restaurants and hotels along the shores of Southwest Florida. She brushed off his reticence as humbleness about his family's money. There was a strong mutual physical attraction between them; it was clear Sean's focus was on her.

MIDNIGHT PASS

They had finished the bottle of wine and locked in a deep embrace and deeper kiss Haley's elbow absently knocked the bottle over. It rolled across the deck in a looping arc and went overboard. They broke the kiss and laughed, their faces awash with lavender under the exterior lighting. The bottle bobbed twice and disappeared under the moonlit surface.

"Oh shit," Haley giggled.

Sean was laughing, "Down with the fishes she goes."

Looking at the water Haley asked, "How deep is it here?"

Sean shrugged once. "Maybe twenty-five feet."

Haley looked up from the water and scanned the line of dark beach. She could not see anyone out and there were now fewer lights on the shore. The yacht's lighting reflected on the water, dancing brilliant violet across the easy peaks and troughs. Haley slipped her phone from her back pocket and checked the time. Two minutes to midnight.

It was later than she thought. She pocketed her cell and was about to comment on the time when a sound caught her ear, an engine out on the water, coming from the south. The whining pitch was closing on them. Haley turned to look but didn't see anything at first. As the vessel drew closer Haley could see in the ambient lighting it was a jet ski, dark, no running lights, heading towards them. Riding the jet ski was a man, and it was clear that he was headed directly for *Midnight Pass.*

Beside her Sean rose to his feet, also looking at the approaching jet ski. Haley frowned and looked up at Sean. "Do you know him?"

As the man was navigating the watercraft in towards the yacht's stern, Sean said flatly, "Yes, it's my buddy. He's come to join us for some fun."

Haley looked quickly up at Sean. "Your buddy? You invited your friend out here? For some fun? What kind of fun?"

Sean looked down at Haley, his eyes cold steel. "You."

Haley's growing concern hastily turned into surprise, and fear. She started to get to her feet when Sean reeled back and slammed his fist into the side of her jaw. The impact snapped her head around, twisting Haley off balance and she went down hard on the fiberglass decking, knocked out cold.

* * * *

Returning to consciousness, the first thing Haley felt was the terrific pain in her jaw. The right side of her face was throbbing and swollen, and she had a fierce pounding headache. She could taste blood in her mouth and gently pushing her tongue around felt an incisor loose. The inside of her right cheek had been smashed across her teeth and was torn open. Opening her eyes, she saw she was laying on her back on a large bed, in what looked like a yacht's cabin. It was not the stateroom she had looked in on while using the bathroom. This one was larger, but the décor matched.

She was still on *Midnight Pass*.

Haley lifted her head and shifted to try and sit up. She could not move. She was bound, tied by wrist and ankle, spreadeagle. She struggled, feeling a new rising panic. Coming more awake and to her senses, she pulled against the restraints. The ties did not give. She wasn't going anywhere fast. Relaxing her body, Haley took a couple of breaths and studied her binds. She was tied with white braided nautical line, wrapped and knotted tightly around her wrists, pulling her arms overhead, the ropes going up and behind the bed's headboard. The same line was bound around her ankles, going off the edge of the bed. The rope had very little give when she pulled against the restraints. Whomever had tied her had experience with lines and knots and had done a damn good job.

Haley was barefoot and she also noticed that her blouse was torn open, and her bra askew. Feeling anger swell up, Haley again tugged hard against her restraints and struggled to sit up. She got nowhere and her headache turned into a blinding agony.

Haley tried to recall the evening. On top of the concussion, she also had drunk a few large glasses of wine, and was only realizing now that her thoughts were slow and memory blurry: the dock, the yacht, meeting Sean, anchoring in the Gulf, red wine, kissing . . . From there it went dark. They were sitting out on the bow, making out. Her memories of the night swirled into a dark void. She had woken with her face injured and bound on a bed in what looked to be the master stateroom.

She looked around the cabin. The bed was large, elevated, with modern side tables and the walls were dark wood paneling. Recessed lights in the ceiling lit the stateroom well. Beyond the foot of the bed were two closets on either side of the room, and a long window between showing only the black of night. Tipping her head back she could see the same dark window over the headboard. The large stateroom ran the full beam of the yacht. Along the wall to her left was a long bookshelf holding a run of paperbacks. On the opposite wall was a framed photograph, an aerial shot of a sleek white yacht cruising over gin-clear turquoise water. The name, *Midnight Pass*, was clearly visible on the stern transom. To the right was the cabin doorway, left open, leading to the main hallway with the bow cabin and head Haley used, and the stairs heading up to the salon above her.

Haley remembered her phone. Her cell had been in the back pocket of her shorts. She twisted to her right side, pushing her butt cheek down against the mattress. She could not feel any bump, her phone was no longer in her pocket.

It was then, from the hallway, she could hear muffled

voices from above deck. Two men, one voice she recognized as Sean's and another she didn't know. Haley focused and realized she could just make out what they were saying, over the low sound of music. The second man seemed to be riding Sean for something.

* * * *

Up in the salon Sean sat on the couch and watched his friend Pat down the rest of his beer. Sean and Pat, both now twenty-seven, had known each other since grade school, long-time buddies who grew up together, living the Florida lifestyle: fishing, boating, the beach. They also shared another dark passion, abusing girls. It started off slow, at first, in high school, which they blew off as just harmless fun. Forcing a girl to do things she didn't want to do. Over the years it progressed rapidly, to the two of them abducting young women, full on kidnapping, restraint, rape. The crazy thing was they also got away with it. Easily. Afterwards they would give the girl a heavy dose of a benzodiazepine or chloral hydrate, or both, and then drop her somewhere inconspicuous. There was never any news or sign of a report or story from the girls, and Sean and Pat always got away scot-free.

Both came from wealthy families, Sean still lived right in Englewood where his parents owned and ran several prominent restaurants and a marina. Sean's father was a lecherous rake who cheated on his wife and enjoyed the services of young escorts when he was away on business and fishing trips. The apple did not fall far from the tree with his son. Except Sean took his own depravity to a new sublevel, far crossing the line.

For the past few years Pat had a condo up in Tampa and a growing addiction he was nurturing well, sports betting.

Specifically on fights, boxing and UFC. And right now, Pat was on the tail end of a bad losing streak, in deep with his bookie.

Pat was a bit shorter than Sean, and burlier, with sandy blond hair, gray eyes, and a 'good ol' boy' face and personality; polite, charming, friendly. Tonight, Pat's face was strained with worry. He was wearing sun-faded gray board shorts and a black Salt Life rash guard. He had slammed through the Corona Sean had pulled for him from the galley fridge.

When Sean and Haley had gone out onto the bow Sean had quickly sent a text to Pat, and his friend had made his way out to *Midnight Pass* on his Sea Doo from where he was waiting at the Indian Mound Park boat ramp. Sean knew he had the hook set in deep with this girl Haley, luring her with charm, guile, and persuasion out onto the yacht, and he and Pat were going to have some fun with her. But tonight, Pat was off, distracted and concerned with gambling debts he had accumulated. The past few days, since the end of the weekend, Pat had been staying in Englewood at his parents' place, ducking his bookie in Tampa.

"Look," Pat was saying, setting his empty bottle on the salon table, "I know your dad has some money on this boat— cash that your mom doesn't know about. Fun money, for when he's out cruising with the boys on long weekender trips down to Sanibel and the Keys. Money for partying, for girls. I need to borrow it."

"You've got to be fucking kidding," Sean shook his head, "No way. If my dad ever found out any of that money was missing—"

"He won't find out, I'll get it back before he ever knows it's gone," Pat's voice was underscored with strain. "I need to pay Marco, and I need to pay him now."

"Man, I can't let you have that money."

"I really gotta pay this guy Sean, I swear I can get the

money back before your dad finds out. I only need it for a few days, to tide Marco over for a bit. I'm in trouble man, like big trouble. He's been threatening to send a couple of his cronies after me—like serious 'break my legs' kinda shit. I think he's even had them tail me to Englewood. I've seen them, watching me. A couple of severe badasses—Ukrainians."

Sean snorted. "All right, now you're just getting paranoid. You owe this guy some money but he's not going to have you fuckin' killed dude."

Pat slapped his hands on his thighs in frustration and stood up, crossing into the galley. "I've met these guys before, in Tampa—Marco's muscle—you have no idea, you don't want to fuck with them. Shit man, I need another beer."

* * * *

Below decks Haley lay still and listened to the exchange between Sean and this guy Pat. As far as she knew, Pat was not onboard when they left the dock. It was then she remembered the jet ski, the watercraft approaching the yacht. Sean had known that this man Pat was coming. And then it all went dark.

Haley started to become furious with herself, furious that she could let herself get into a situation like this—she was too astute to get caught up in this kind of trouble. But here she was, tied up and held captive on a boat like some dumb character victim in a bad movie. Her smarts had not paid off, not in this scenario. Haley still trusted and believed all people were inherently good. That was her fatal flaw.

She started to frantically work her wrists and ankles, twisting and turning and pulling against her binds. They were not loosening at all, in fact, the knots were tightening. The cord bit into her skin and chafed until she saw the skin around her wrist peel back and there was a seeping of blood. Head pounding, jaw aching, and the coppery taste of blood still slick in her sore mouth, Haley quit fighting the restraints. She lay slack on the bed in the luxuriant master stateroom and listened to the men above her.

* * * *

"You're not getting it," Pat's voice was becoming more desperate. He had got himself another Corona from the galley fridge and was leaning against the marble counter. "This is serious, I'm in over my head. Way over my head."

Sean's tone was sedate. "How much?"

Pat looked up at his friend, and after a minute, shaking his head, he answered weightily, "Eighty grand."

"Holy Christ! Eighty fuckin' grand! How in the hell did you get in that big of a hole?"

Pat shook his head again and took a long pull on the beer. Setting the bottle on the counter he looked up at Sean. "Two weeks ago, I went in heavy . . . put five dimes on the big fight—on that beast Carnera—his win was gonna make me back what I lost the week before—he was a surefire lock to take out Willis. But the fucker went down—KO'd in the first goddamn round. Willis toppled him. I'm screwed."

"Shit man," Sean let out a breath, "What're you going to do?"

"I don't know. Marco has been cool, but this is too much. I've pushed him to his limit and now over." Pat looked his friend in the eye. "I could really use that money."

Sean's face was hard as he struggled with the decision to help his friend out with his father's money. They both knew Sean's dad indeed kept a small horde of cash on *Midnight Pass*. But if his dad ever found out Sean had touched that money . . .

Pat saw Sean's indecision and pushed on. "I just need it for a few days. I can have it back on the boat by Friday night—no later than Saturday. Your dad has no plans to take the boat out before then?"

Sean slowly shook his head.

"Then there won't be a problem. Again, I'm serious, I really gotta pay Marco or I'm going to find myself in a spot I can't walk away from."

Sean twirled his beer atop a cork coaster on the salon table. "How're you going to get the money back by Saturday?"

Pat saw his friend was caving. "I have a loan being approved this week at the bank, I'll use it first to pay back your father's cash, and the rest will go to the balance I owe Marco."

"What's the loan amount? I've never seen my dad have more than forty grand onboard."

"Fifty." Pat wasn't lying, but it was a stretch of the truth. It was unlikely the Bank of America in town was going to approve a line of credit application for fifty thousand dollars with his banking history. "Forty goes back to your dad, and the rest on to Marco. Fifty G's is more than half of my debt, that'll satisfy him and get these guys off my back."

Sean did not look thrilled with this plan and was struggling with indecision. "Fuck." He tipped back the last of his Corona. "Alright. But you absolutely gotta have that cash back on this boat by Saturday."

Pat let out a sigh of relief. "No problem. Thanks brother, I really needed this help."

"By Saturday night," Sean repeated loud and clear.

"I got it, sure," Pat replied, his ease and mood shifting gears, "Look, let's forget it for now. Tonight's our night for some fun, isn't it? Who is this girl again? I didn't get a good look at her as you were dragging her below."

"Some Ivy League bitch, from New York. She's hot and she's going to be a sport."

"Nice. You met her at SandBar?"

"Mm-hmm. And that's where were gonna drop her, late, after we give her a Mickey Finn."

Pat grinned, "Alright, let's have a look."

They got up and Pat followed Sean down the steps from the salon to the cabins.

＊ ＊ ＊ ＊

Haley's heart was hammering inside her chest, and she was frozen with fear. She had again started working and struggling non-stop to free herself while listening to the men talk upstairs, and had managed to loosen one wrist, slightly. Blood stained the white line tied around her hand. Now she was motionless in terror as she heard the two of them coming for her, down the steps, down the hallway, and into the master stateroom . . .

Sean and Pat stood in the cabin doorway, eyeing her.

"Look who's awake," said Sean.

"Well hell, aren't you going to be a ball," Pat goaded as he looked Haley up and down. He glanced at Sean. "She's fucking hot alright, but you did a number to her face."

Pat crossed the cabin and stepped towards the end of the bed. He reached down and grasped Haley's foot. At his touch Haley jumped and started pulling hard against all four binds, twisting her ankle away from his hand.

Haley's voice broke ragged and hoarse, "Don't you fucking touch me."

Adrenaline, anger, and fright coursed through her body. She looked from Pat to Sean. "You asshole—let me go."

Sean snickered and came around the side of the bed.

"You're far too trusting sweety. You shouldn't be going out on boats with strange guys."

Haley glared at Sean, sickened by the sight of him as he came closer. "You let me fucking go right now."

"Right," Sean pushed and provoked, "We'll let you go, but first we're all gonna have some fun. The three of us."

Grinning madly, Pat came around the other side of the bed, running his hand from her foot up her leg, his other hand rubbing his crotch.

"You fucking assholes!" Haley hissed. She was pulling harder than ever on her wrists, tearing the skin. She did not feel any pain, but the binds were loosening further. Just not yet nearly enough to slip a hand free. There was no doubt in her panicked mind; these sadists were going to rape her.

Pat leaned over Haley and pulled hard at her blouse, tearing it down and open in one savage tug. His hand went for her bra, cupping a breast, squeezing hard. They were on each side of her and she was pinned, helpless, defenseless. A hand was rough between her legs. Panic and terror welled up in her again and she closed her eyes.

"What the fuck was that?" Sean's voice, anxious and uneasy.

"What the fuck was what?" Pat replied, his focus entirely on Haley's breasts.

"*Shh*!" Sean looked up and studied the roof of the cabin. His voice was low, "I heard something—against the hull."

"What?" Pat asked, irritated by the distraction. "It's probably just the Sea Doo."

"No," Sean was stepping back from the bed, moving towards the cabin door. "I don't think so."

Pat straightened up and looked down at Haley with an expression of pure rancor. "If you make a sound—I will kill you."

Haley stayed silent. She watched as Pat moved away,

stepping lightly around the foot of the bed to Sean, both standing at the open cabin doorway, looking down the hall.

Sean dropped his head back towards Pat and spoke under his breath, "Someone's on the fucking boat."

Pat turned and glared at Haley and put a finger to his lips. She didn't move.

"Shit," Sean breathed, unsure what to do. He strained his ears. The radio in the salon was masking any subtle sounds if anyone was up there. He looked at Pat, his voice low. "I'm gonna go check it out, you stay with her."

Pat nodded, feeling a growing worry in his gut. He watched Sean edge down the shadowy LED lit hallway and open the polished teak door that opened to the main hallway. The main hallway held the day head Haley had used, and the VIP stateroom she had peaked in on at the bow. Sean stuck his head around the door and looked aft, towards the stairs, up to the salon.

There was a rushing blur from the stairs, and Sean's world went black.

From the cabin doorway Pat watched as Sean collapsed to the floor. Pat froze for a second, not knowing what happened, or what to do. The door was yanked open wide, and a man stepped over Sean and into the stateroom hallway. He was holding a matte black pistol, aimed right at Pat's chest. Pat immediately recognized Luca, hired muscle working for his bookie Marco.

"Shit . . ." Pat moaned.

Luca was tall, lanky, and dark eyed, gray skin with a few days' growth of stubble, and thick unruly hair. He was in a short sleeve button-down cream-colored shirt, jeans, and black alligator skin shoes. Luca motioned with the handgun, "Let's go."

Without looking back at Haley Pat moved towards Luca, up the hallway. He slowly held up his hands, "Luca, listen—"

"Pick him up." Luca ignored Pat and motioned down to Sean.

Pat looked down at his friend. Sean had a nasty gash on his forehead where Luca had whacked him with the pistol. He bent and slipped his hands under Sean's arms, hefting the dead weight.

Luca backed through the door into the main hallway. "Bring him up the stairs."

Pat grunted and hoisted Sean up. Sean made a sound; he was slowly coming to. As Pat heaved his friend up the stairs into the salon, his mind raced about what he was going to say to diffuse this situation—there was the cash on the boat. He had already forgotten about Haley, she no longer mattered.

Pat's heart dropped when he saw a second man he knew as Volkov standing in the middle of the salon, holding a baseball bat. The second half of Marco's muscle. Volkov was not tall and lanky, he was a brick shithouse. He looked just like what an Eastern European hired gunman should look like. Intimidating as hell. Shaved head covered in tattoos, arms like Schwarzenegger's in the 80s, and face like a bulldog. The bat was wood, and glinted midnight black.

Pat knew he had seen both Luca and Volkov here in Englewood just a day ago. He wasn't paranoid, they had been tailing him. Pat dragged Sean into the salon and left him lying on the laminate flooring in a state of semi-consciousness.

"We missed you at the boat ramp," Luca jeered in heavily accented English. "Which is bad for you, because Volkov hates going out on the water. He hates boats."

"Look—" Pat raised a hand, "I have half the money right now, tonight." He was relieved to see Sean coming to.

Sean was working on sitting up and put a hand to his head. It came away covered in blood. He looked up bleary-eyed and confused at the sight Luca and Volkov. His eyes quickly found the gun and the baseball bat. "Who're you guys? What are you doing on my boat?"

Luca laughed. "This is your daddy's boat, not yours. And your friend here owes us money."

Pat said, "I was just telling them we have half the money Sean, right now, here—on the boat."

Sean grimaced from the wound to his head, further took in the situation and nodded. "Yeah, I have at least half of what Pat owes this guy—" Sean struggled to recall the name, "—Marco. Forty thousand."

Luca laughed and shook his head. "Unfortunately, Marco didn't send us here tonight to collect any money. He sent us to collect, but you're paying in pain and blood, not cash."

Pat felt a jolt of fear course through him. "I have half of what I owe Marco—I can pay you right now." He looked quickly over at his friend. "Sean—where is the money?"

Sean glanced down the stairs and then back at Luca. "It's in the master cabin. I can get it." He made to get up and Volkov stepped forward with the bat.

Luca spoke menacingly, "It's too late for half payments and empty promises. Marco wants me to inform you your debt to him is no longer eighty . . . it's now one hundred thousand. And it's due Saturday, all of it. We're here to remind you of what happens when you renege on your debts." Luca looked at Volkov and nodded once.

Volkov moved towards Pat, raising the baseball bat.

"Wait!" Pat yelled, raising both hands and stepping back, "Christ, we have the money, I told you—"

The end of the bat caught Pat in the gut, causing him to double over and let out a long wheezing gasp. He dropped to his knees; arms wrapped around his stomach. The second swing landed across his left upper arm, cracking the humerus and toppling him over into the dining table.

Sean watched in shock, helplessly from the floor in the galley, flinching repeatedly as Volkov swung the bat a half dozen times on his friend. Volkov muttered a few expletives in Ukrainian as he hammered away. Cowering on the Bertram's flooring, it looked to Sean like Pat had lost consciousness. A swing had taken him on the side of his head, splitting open the skin, and his face was already swelling and quickly patterning a dark maroon. Pat was pale and his eyes were open, pupils fixed and dilated. Blood ran from an ear.

"Alright, alright, Christ—don't kill him," Luca stepped forward and pulled Volkov back by an arm, slipping the pistol into the waistband of his pants. He looked down at Sean. "OK, you tell your friend to pay, huh?" Luca looked from Sean to Volkov and nodded. "Make sure he doesn't forget. Not as bad as his friend though, don't hit his arms too much—he needs to drive the boat."

Volkov grinned like an ogre and turned to Sean. The baseball bat was running slick with dark crimson.

"Wait!" Sean wailed, starting to tremble, "Wait! I can pay you right now—"

The bat cut him off as Volkov set to work on his legs. Sean's screams turned to mewling whimpers as he writhed on the floor in agony under the fall of the bat. After six solid swings Volkov stepped back. Sean was quivering on the floor, arms held across his face, moaning.

"Let's go," Luca grunted, "It's an hour and a half drive back to Tampa, and it's already past midnight."

The Ukrainians left *Midnight Pass* as quickly and silently as they had boarded. Neither Sean nor Pat had seen the vessel they arrived on, and the two henchmen disappeared into the night.

MIDNIGHT PASS

* * * *

Haley had lain stock-still in terror, listening to everything. She had heard the first thump as Sean hit the floor in the master stateroom hallway just six minutes ago. She had also clearly heard the loud double thump directly overhead as Pat fell onto his knees and hit the floor. Followed closely by Sean's pathetic squeals. From the resounding above it appeared both Pat and Sean were beaten, and both possibly unconscious. The radio in the salon had been switched off, there were no other sounds, just an unnerving new silence as *Midnight Pass* pulled gently and swung on her anchor line. The wind from the west had picked up a few knots.

A dozen times she had almost decided to call out, but hearing the events taking place above, erred on the side of caution and silence. She had no idea who the two European sounding men were, but knew they were dangerous, possibly even more dangerous than Sean and Pat. From the sounds of what had transpired, she had guessed right.

With renewed vigor she began working to free herself, twisting and turning her wrists and ankles. After a couple of minutes her right foot unexpectedly jerked up and free as whatever the rope had been tied to under the bed broke loose. One leg was out. Encouraged, she worked her right wrist savagely, the blood from her shredding skin lubricating the bind.

Another couple of minutes of biting pain paid off. Haley's wrist slipped through the line with a stinging brutal pop, and she let out a yelp at both the intense burning sensation and freedom. With her right hand she set to work on her left wrist, and it only took a minute to undo the ties holding her. Sitting up on the bed she bent forward and ignored the pulsing headache as she freed her left ankle.

She was loose.

Eyes wide, breathing heavily, Haley sat still and listened. Still no movement from above, only silence.

She swung her legs off the bed, the flooring was cool on the soles of her bare feet. Standing wearily and finding her balance she took stock, blouse torn open and hanging off a shoulder. The only way off the yacht was up the stairs and through the salon . . . right past where it sounded like Sean and Pat were beaten unconscious. She crossed to the cabin door and saw the hallway was empty. She was about to set out down the hall when she remembered the exchange between Sean and Pat, speaking with the men.

". . . we have half the money, right now, here—on the boat. Forty thousand. I can pay you right now. Sean—where is the money?"

"It's in the master cabin. I can get it."

Haley froze, turned her head, and slowly looked around the stateroom. Where would there be forty thousand dollars in the bedroom? Should she risk the time to look? How long would it take her to find it? Forty grand . . .

Haley started with the bedside tables and found nothing but back issues of boating magazines, a watch, perfume, hand lotion and not much else. She tried the cedar-lined closets and found some clothing: shirts, a hoodie, rash guards, pants, both men's and women's shoes and sandals. The large pull-out storage drawers under the elevated bed were entirely empty. Haley stood and her eyes fell along the bookshelf on the stern wall.

A line of paperbacks and a few hardbacks held in place by a retaining wire across their spines. Coming around the bed Haley examined the books, mostly all of them from the same author whose name she recognized—John Cannon—thrillers with a Florida setting. Haley began tipping the books out, tumbling them onto the floor. She watched the titles scatter: *Casperson Sands, Everglades City, Shark Valley.*

With the bookshelf cleared and not revealing anything, Haley felt her frustration rise. The clock was ticking. She was about to turn from the empty shelf when she noticed the floor of the bookshelf had a cut-out with a small metal latch that could be flipped up to slide a finger through. She quickly pried it up to reveal a small cubby recessed under the bookshelf. Inside was a paper bag.

Haley lifted out the bag out and opened it up. Inside were four wrapped bundles of hundreds, in the mustard yellow American Bankers Association currency band marked $10,000. One of the bands had been tapped into a bit, but Haley guessed she had close to forty thousand dollars. Enough to pay her grandmother's rent at the condo for almost three years. She also noticed inside the bag was a slip of notepad paper. Pulling it out, written in ballpoint ink, she read the names of three girls— Chrissy, Tegan, Jade—and their respective phone numbers. Haley slipped the notepaper back into the bag and scrunched it closed.

About to bail out of the cabin, at the bottom of the hidden cubby another slip of paper caught her eye. This one was letter-size, with printed type and a business card paper-clipped to the top left corner. Haley picked the paper up and scanned it. It was the registration for the yacht; purchased for $3.4 million last October at the Fort Lauderdale Boat Show. At the top was the client's name, which Haley deduced was Sean's father, Martin Russell. She had his name: Sean Russell. It also had a home address in Englewood and phone number. The business card was for a yacht broker from MarineMax.

Haley's mind was running in overdrive. Would it not be a treat to call up Chrissy and Tegan and Jade and have them pay a special surprise visit to Sean's father, this time not out on his fancy yacht, but at home? He might have trouble paying the girls, as his 'fun money' was now going to be covering her grandmother's rent.

Haley shoved the registration paper into the bag, and not even thinking to look for her shoes, turned and exited the cabin. Silently she slipped around the teak door into the main passage. At the base of the stairs, she paused and looked up into the salon. It looked empty, no movement or sound. Padding barefoot without a sound up the stairs, she immediately saw both Sean and Pat laying on the floor of the salon. They were not moving. Haley glanced over at Pat. He was out cold, laying facedown beside a scattered table and chairs, and looked to be in even worse condition than Sean. He had taken a far more severe beating. His face was bashed black and blue, one eye swollen shut, and blood trickled out of an ear. Haley could see from the alignment of one of his arms it was broken in at least a couple of places.

Stepping carefully up into the salon, Haley crept around Sean. He was laying on his left side, head on the floor. Her heart spiked adrenaline when she saw his eyes were open—he was awake, looking up at her. Sean tried to move and hissed with pain.

"Help me—" he gasped between labored pained breaths, "—get me my phone."

Looking down at him she took a couple of steps closer to Sean, until she was just a foot from his head.

"Fuck you," Haley spat, and in one solid motion brought her leg up and stomped her bare heel down on his face, breaking his nose. She felt the cartilage pop and slide under her foot. Sean snorted blood and groaned like a stuck pig.

MIDNIGHT PASS

Haley saw her phone sitting on the galley's marble countertop. She snatched it up, brought up her camera and snapped a few photos of Sean, and then Pat. Sean was trying to say something but only bubbled crimson blood from his busted nose.

"Fuck you motherfucker. Burn in hell." Haley's voice was acid.

The clock on her phone screen read 12:33 a.m. She pocketed her cell, turned from the men on the floor and pressed through the salon to the rear door. Sliding it open . . . she was outside, in the humid night air, the warm teak decking under her feet. Taking a few deep breaths she scanned the beach off the stern, just a dark line to the east, only a few lights on now, a thousand feet of black water to the sand. Her full intention was to swim it, until she saw the jet ski. Pat's black and teal Sea Doo sat alongside the stern of *Midnight Pass*, tethered to the cleats on the transom.

Gripping the paper bag, Haley climbed over the gunwale and down onto the jet ski, feeling it bob and roll under her weight. She was somewhat familiar with jet skis, having ridden them a couple of times off Long Island. Situating herself on the watercraft she popped open the storage compartment between her legs and tossed in the bag. She unwound the mooring lines and pushed away from *Midnight Pass*. The Sea Doo started on a nudge of the ignition button, and the watercraft immediately started to idle forward.

Haley gave the craft some throttle and the jet ski plowed ahead and away from the stern of the yacht. Holding on and acquiring the feel, she gave it another hit of fuel and carved a wide turn, circling around and heading east. The Sea Doo made quick work of the gap between *Midnight Pass* and the shore of Englewood Beach.

The wind and sea spray whipped Haley's hair and her torn blouse flapped behind her. The salt stung her cut lip, and she felt an overwhelming sense of exhilaration, relief, and thankfulness. Sean and Pat had gotten their just desserts. She had escaped, she had survived, and she had won. With a little help from two men named Luca and Volkov. Haley did not want to fathom what would have happened to her if those two had discovered her tied up below decks. Would they have freed her, or were they as sadistic and rapine as Sean and Pat?

Haley let off the gas as she approached the surf line, and the waves pushed the jet ski in towards the beach. The Sea Doo slid up onto the sand and she cut the throttle, beaching the watercraft. Haley got her bearings; she had come onto the public town beach just north of the main pavilion. Across a wide swath of sand lit by the full moon, a boardwalk ran the length of the beach through a maze of sabal palms, behind a rise of dunes covered in sea oats. Inside the witching hour the beach was dark and appeared deserted.

Haley cut the engine and flipped open the lid of the storage compartment. Grabbing her reward, she stepped off the jet ski into ankle-deep surf. She turned and looked back out into the Gulf at *Midnight Pass*. The yacht's fancy violet night lighting was now turned off, only a single masthead light was on and some muted cabin light through the windows. There was no sign of movement onboard. Haley surmised that neither of the duo were going anywhere soon, if at all, without help.

She was making her way up the beach, her moon shadow tracking across the flat sand ahead of her, when a voice spoke out in the darkness.

"Out for a midnight ride?"

Haley almost jumped out of her skin. Her nervous system was still wound wire tight and would be for quite some time.

She looked to her left to see the silhouette of a man standing on the beach about fifteen feet away. He was just standing relaxed under the starlight, looking out into the Gulf. He must have watched her beach the Sea Doo, but she had not seen him coming in. Did he see her leave from the yacht? The jet ski did not have any running lights, she came in dark.

"Yeah," Haley replied curtly, and made to continue up the beach.

"Lucky you. Nice night for a ride." His voice had a native southern accent, and Haley caught a whiff of stale beer and cigarettes.

The man was Ken Bowden, a forty-seven-year-old semi-homeless down-and-out, born and raised in Englewood, and known around town as a harmless derelict. He lived squatting in a tent on vacant land and parks, always out and about on his bike, with a smoke clamped between his few remaining teeth, skin tanned a deep mahogany. Ken was a regular at the AA meetings in Indian Mound Park, usually attending only after he had had a few beers, and then mostly for the company, and cookies.

"Hey, are you alright?" he asked, genuine concern in his tone, "You're looking a little rough . . . did y'all have an accident out there?"

Sean had belted her good. Haley could only guess what she looked like until she found a mirror. She also remembered that her blouse was ripped open and falling off one shoulder. "I'm alright," she remarked, self-consciously pulling her shirt up.

"You sure?"

Haley paused her advance up the sloped pan. She turned to the man and nodded. "Yes, thank you."

"You ain't from around here, are ya'? You from up north?"

Haley nodded.

"Well, welcome to Florida."

Haley let out an exhausted sardonic laugh. Sean had said the same thing to her at SandBar last night. She nodded once more and started to make her way up the beach again.

"Hey, wait—you just gonna leave that jet ski sitting there like that?"

Haley looked back over her shoulder, glancing first at the Sea Doo and then at the man. "It's yours if you want it."

Ken stared at her blankly for a moment. "You kidding?"

Haley shook her head, turned, and continued up the beach.

Ken chuckled and watched Haley ascend the stairs to the pavilion at the top of the sand. The girl did not stop or look back and she disappeared into the night.

"Huh," Ken shrugged in disbelief, slowly shaking his head. He turned to look at the Sea Doo beached on the pan. He walked over and laid a palm on the handlebar. Pausing first to look up and down the beach, and then back at the pavilion where the girl had departed, he pushed the jet ski back off the sand and into the surf. Moving the gently pitching Sea Doo into knee-deep water, Ken stepped onto the watercraft. Hitting the start button the engine sprang to life, exhaust bubbling and sputtering saltwater, and the Sea Doo idled forward.

"I'll be damned," Ken muttered to himself, the weeks' worth of stubble on his face cracking into a huge grin, "Welcome to Florida, indeed."

He hit the throttle and the jet ski shot forward, riding hard and fast out on the dark Gulf waters.

AUTHOR'S NOTE

Thank you for reading my novella, *Midnight Pass*. I hope you enjoyed the story, and if you did, I thank you again for taking just a minute to leave a review on Amazon. As an independently published author support from readers is crucial, and positive reviews help to get exposure. I love to hear from my readers, so feel free to reach out to me via the CONTACT page on my website. Thanks again, and I'll see you inside another story soon!

To receive news and updates on future novels sign up for my newsletter here: www.toddcameron.net/newsletter

Find my books on Amazon: www.amazon.com/Todd-Cameron/e/B0979CKVP4

Connect on Facebook: www.facebook.com/toddcameronauthor

Follow on Instagram: www.instagram.com/toddcameronauthor

ABOUT THE AUTHOR

Todd Cameron was born in Montreal, Canada in 1974 and raised in small town rural Ontario. His early pursuits were athletic—skateboarding, bodybuilding, swimming—before finally settling down and focusing on writing, a passion he has had since childhood. Todd has owned and operated a shark diving venture, and he is a certified ocean lifeguard, scuba diver, and swim coach. He completed a 2300 km swim distance challenge to raise awareness for sharks, swimming the same length as the Great Barrier Reef. He competed successfully in open water swimming in the U.S., Canada, Australia, and the Caribbean. Todd enjoys reading, movies, nature, fitness, travel, and being out on the water. He lives in Southwest Florida.

WWW.TODDCAMERON.NET
FB & IG: @TODDCAMERONAUTHOR

Made in the USA
Columbia, SC
27 January 2023

10589819R00033